In a Dark, Dark Room

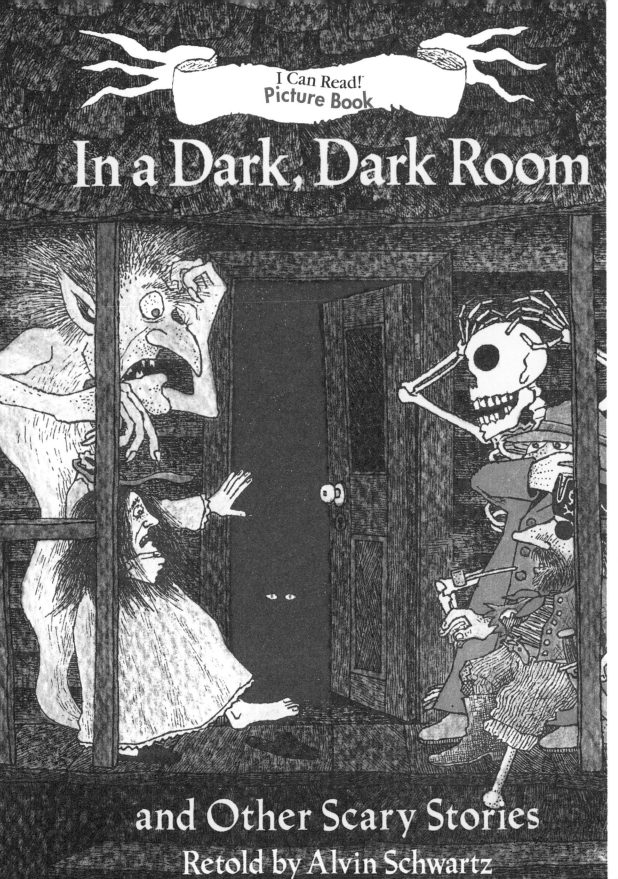

In a Dark, Dark Room

and Other Scary Stories

Retold by Alvin Schwartz
Illustrated by Dirk Zimmer

BARNES & NOBLE

NEW YORK

In a Dark, Dark Room and Other Scary Stories

Text copyright © 1984 by Alvin Schwartz
Illustrations copyright © 1984 by Dirk Zimmer

This 2009 edition licensed for publication by Barnes & Noble Publishing, Inc., by
HarperCollins Publishers.

HarperCollins Publishers ® is a registered trademark.

Barnes & Noble Publishing, Inc.
122 Fifth Avenue
New York, NY 10011

ISBN 13: 978-1-4351-0776-2
ISBN 10: 1-4351-0776-4

Manufactured in China

09 10 11 MCH 10 9 8 7 6 5 4 3 2

To Calliope

Contents

Foreword

Most of us like scary stories

because we *like* feeling scared.

When there is no real danger,

feeling scared is fun.

The best time for these stories

is at night—

in front of a fire or in the dark.

Tell them s-l-o-w-l-y

and quietly,

and everyone will have

a good time.

The Teeth

His teeth were three inches long!

When I saw them, I ran.

When I saw his teeth, I ran.

14

I took one look,

and I ran all the way home.

17

In the Graveyard

A woman in a graveyard sat.

Ooooh!

Very short and very fat.

Ooooh!

She saw three corpses carried in.

Ooooh!

Very tall and very thin.

Ooooh!

To the corpses, the woman said,

"Will I be like you

when I am dead?"

Ooooh!

To the woman, the corpses said,

"You will be like us

when you are dead."

Ooooh!

To the corpses, the woman said,

22

"AAAAAAAAAAAH!"

23

The Green Ribbon

There was a boy named Alfred
in her class.

Alfred liked Jenny,
and Jenny liked Alfred.

One day he asked her,

"Why do you wear that ribbon

all the time?"

"I cannot tell you," said Jenny.

But Alfred kept asking,

"Why *do* you wear it?"

And Jenny would say,

"It is not important."

Jenny and Alfred grew up

and fell in love.

One day they got married.

After their wedding,

Alfred said,

"Now that we are married,

you must tell me

about the green ribbon."

"You still must wait,"

said Jenny.

"I will tell you

when the right time comes."

Years passed.

Alfred and Jenny grew old.

One day Jenny became very sick.

30

The doctor told her

she was dying.

Jenny called Alfred to her side.

31

"Alfred," she said,

"now I can tell you

about the green ribbon.

Untie it,

and you will see

why I could not tell you before."

Slowly and carefully,

Alfred untied the ribbon,

and Jenny's head fell off.

In a Dark, Dark Room

In a dark, dark wood,

there was a dark, dark house.

And in that dark, dark house,

there was a dark, dark room.

And in that dark, dark room,

there was a dark, dark chest.

And in that dark, dark chest,

there was a dark, dark shelf.

And on that dark, dark shelf,

there was a dark, dark box.

And in that dark, dark box,

there was—

A GHOST!

The Night It Rained

It was late at night.

I was driving past the cemetery

when I saw a boy

standing in the rain.

"Do you want a ride home?"

I asked.

"Yes, please," he said.

"I live on Front Street,

next to the school."

I handed him my old sweater.

"It is cold tonight," I said,

"and you are wet.

You had better put this on."

After that, we did not talk.

When we stopped at his house,

I said,

"Keep the sweater.

I will get it tomorrow.

What is your name?"

"Jim," he said.

"Thanks for the ride."

45

I stopped for the sweater

the next day.

A woman came to the door.

"Is Jim at home?" I asked.

"I have come

to pick up my sweater."

46

She looked at me

in a strange way.

"It must have been another boy,"

she said.

"Jim is our son.

But he has been dead

for almost a year.

He is buried in the cemetery."

I told her how sorry I was,

and I left.

I did not know what to think.

The next morning

I went to the cemetery.

I wanted to see Jim's grave.

Lying across the grave

was my sweater.

The Pirate

Ruth was spending her vacation
with her cousin Susan.

"A pirate once lived in our house,"

Susan told Ruth.

"He died in the room

where you are staying.

His ghost is supposed

to haunt that room.

But we have never seen it."

"I don't believe in ghosts,"

said Ruth.

But the thought of a pirate

haunting her room

scared her a little.

Before she got into bed that night,

Ruth looked everywhere.

She looked under the bed

and under the rug,

in the closet

and in the
drawers,

54

behind the dresser

and behind the curtains,

and anywhere else a ghost might hide.

But she did not find a thing.

Ruth yawned and stretched

and got into bed.

She turned off the light

and snuggled under the covers.

"Just as I thought,"

she said to herself.

"There is no one in this room

but me."

Then a big voice said,

"And *ME!*"

WHERE THE STORIES COME FROM

"The Teeth" is based on a story from Surinam (Dutch Guiana) collected in the 1920s by Melville and Frances Herskovitz.

"In the Graveyard" is a short version of the traditional song "Old Woman All Skin and Bone."

"The Green Ribbon" is based on a European folk motif in which a red thread is worn around a person's neck. The thread marks the place where the head was cut off, then reattached.

"In a Dark, Dark Room" is known in England and America.

"The Night It Rained" is based on variants of the widespread folktale "The Ghostly Hitchhiker."

"The Pirate" is based on a reference in *A Dictionary of British Folk-Tales in the English Language* by Katharine M. Briggs, v. 3, p. 416.

"The Ghost of John" was collected by the compiler in 1979 from Lynette M. Lee, age 8, Stockton, California.

ABOUT THE AUTHOR

Alvin Schwartz compiled over two dozen books of folklore for young readers that explores everything from wordplay and humor to tales and legends of all kinds. His books include TOMFOOLERY: *Trickery and Foolery with Words;* A TWISTER OF TWISTS, A TANGLER OF TONGUES; FLAPDOODLE: *Pure Nonsense from American Folklore;* and I SAW YOU IN THE BATHTUB *and Other Folk Rhymes* (an I Can Read Book); his very popular collections of scary stories—SCARY STORIES TO TELL IN THE DARK; MORE SCARY STORIES TO TELL IN THE DARK; SCARY STORIES 3; and the I Can Read Book, GHOSTS!

ABOUT THE ILLUSTRATOR

Dirk Zimmer is a native of Germany who now lives in New York City. He attended the Academie of Fine Arts in Hamburg, Germany, and his work has been shown in private galleries in Switzerland, Germany, and France. Mr. Zimmer has illustrated several children's books, including one he wrote himself: THE TRICK-OR-TREAT TRAP.